Shake Away These Constant Days

Constant Days

30 STORIES
BY RYAN WERNER

Jersey Devil Press
www.jerseydevilpress.com

SHAKE AWAY THESE CONSTANT DAYS

Jersey Devil Press
www.jerseydevilpress.com

Copyright © 2012 by Ryan Werner.
ISBN 978-0-9859062-6-9

FIRST EDITION

Designed by Katie Duffy

The parts of this book that aren't fiction probably aren't about you. Don't make it weird.

Most of these stories previously appeared on the internet as part of the music/literature project Our Band Could Be Your Lit. Some of these stories appeared previously in other places.

"Look At How Fast I Can Go Nowhere At All" at *Amphibi.us*
"This Illusion" in *Prime Number Magazine*
"--:--" in *Fractured West*
"When There Is No Road" at *Literary Fever*

For those about to rock.
And my parents, who bought me my first guitar and my first computer and left me alone long enough to figure out how to use both of them.

TABLE OF CONTENTS

7/Back and to the Left

9/Sergei Avdeyev

12/Look At How Fast I Can Go Nowhere At All

14/The King

19/Plots

21/Wide Right Game

25/When There Is No Road

28/It's Been Far Too Long Since You Woke Up In Someone Else's Shoes

31/Monsters: A Series of Non-Chronological Vignettes

35/Rust

38/The Vikings

42/Signal

44/--:--

46/Haunt

49/After I Threw the Ball At Thomas Hernandez and Before It Killed Him

51/Follow the Water

54/A Few Thoughts on Bloodlines

56/Focus

59/Facts

62/Sweet Tooth

65/What Burns Never Returns

67/Let's Go Shoot Her While She's Crying

71/Jests At Scars

73/This Illusion

76/Where Is Your H?

79/Mythology

82/B Sharp, C Flat

85/Flood

88/Refund

92/Things That Are Glacial, Things That Are Gone

Back and to the Left

Aside from his relations with Marilyn Monroe and being the most powerful man in the United States for a little bit, JFK wasn't the luckiest guy around. He was accident prone, more than anything. Still, he kept his humor. He'd call me a few times a year and say something like, "I just slammed my hand in a car door. First I get shot in the head and now this."

But he's dead now. For real this time.

A few months before that car ride in Dallas, John decided he didn't want to be president anymore, which would have been a hassle in and of itself, but he also decided he didn't want to be JFK anymore, either. There's a paper-trail a few miles long hidden away somewhere, but after it was all said and done, we managed to relocate him to Florida with fewer than half a dozen people knowing about it. He loved Scrabble and was big into anagrams, so he took the name John Zing, which, combined with the words "faked tenderly," have all the same letters as the name John Fitzgerald Kennedy. I can only imagine how long he thought about all this before he finally brought it up to me.

Part of this is a history lesson, and part of it is just history. The guy who got shot was an ex-marine who figured it was a service to the country to let JFK have his way. A little plastic surgery later and he looked good enough to be in public for a few minutes before we shot him. While Jackie was picking up what she thought was the top of her husband's skull, her husband was getting some reconstructive surgery of his own, reshaping his chin, filing down his cheekbones, bending his nose around like silly putty.

Flash forward several decades and John dies of pneumonia. He was in his nineties. He had a pretty Cuban wife—his way of making up for the Bay of Pigs, I guess— and some kids. (He'd send me some pictures every once in a while. That jaw. Goddamn.) Everyone got what they wanted, really. Jackie became a symbol of feminine strength and didn't have a philandering husband anymore. Lyndon Johnson swore in as president. John was free. This is all his rationalizing. He told me that even America got what it wanted: a tragedy to unite it. "Only when consumed with grief can people wrap their arms around one another and be complete," he said. "Like fingers rolling into a fist."

Sergei Avdeyev

'm sitting in a tavern in Moscow drinking by myself
when I look over and see Sergei Avdeyev doing the
same. Folded neatly on the bar stool next to him is a
silver and blue windbreaker. I'm unsure if it's really him,
but as I steal more glances his way, I notice an
embroidered patch with the Russian space program logo
sewn into the sleeve of the jacket. The sun is just starting
to set and more people are filtering in. Still, the tavern is
less than a quarter full. Sergei and I sit at the bar, two of
only a half dozen people to do so. He's sitting there, his
face looking interested but his body looking bored,
hunched over slightly and tinkering with his change.
Every few drinks he rolls his sleeves up a bit further and
smiles modestly, as if he has just thought of an
extraordinary idea.

I've kept up on space the way most men keep up with
sports or politics. During Sergei's tenure as a cosmonaut
he spent a little more than two years in space at about
17,000 miles an hour. He gathered enough speed over the
course of enough time to move one-fiftieth of a second into
the future.

I wave the bartender over. "Is that Sergei Avdeyev?" I
ask.

"Yes, that is Sergei. He comes here often to drink

beers. He is a very quiet, very smart man."

"Do you think I could order him a drink?"

The bartender swipes his thick palm across the top of the bar before walking over to Sergei. Moments later, he's back and telling me that Sergei appreciates my gesture, but he has drunk enough for the night. I look over to Sergei, who is still looking forward, still grinning mildly. All at once, it becomes important that I interact with him, and in my head his presence becomes a reason for celebration, the mild hysteria normally associated with seeing a rock star or an actor. "Ask him if he'd like to play darts with me," I tell the bartender, who again brushes his hand across the bar and then knocks on it twice with his knuckles.

Sergei does not know any English, yet when he walks up to me from across the bar, already holding the darts, he lets me know his appreciation by extending his hand, which is solid and lean, as is everything about him.

I lose three games in a row. I aim for the bull's-eye and hit it once. I'm gasping for technique, switching the fingers I throw with, shifting large handfuls of Russian coins from pocket to pocket trying to find a balance. Toward the end, when our scores are almost even, I keep busting, setting myself back again and again. Sergei throws with his engineer mind and his cosmonaut body: long, accurate tosses from his slender arm, sailing true and adding up to zero every time.

We shake hands again and head back to the bar. There is a brief interaction between the bartender and Sergei, and then Sergei removes his windbreaker from the stool, drapes it over his arm, and waves goodbye to me before leaving. When I order another beer, the bartender tells me that Sergei has bought me three of them, one for each loss in our series of darts. I drink them slowly, and by the time I'm on the last one, the tavern has filled out. People are packed six to a booth. All the stools at the bar are taken, people crammed between them trying to order, trying to carry on a conversation. I finish and make my way through the crowd and out the door. Instead of hailing a taxi, I run, weaving through the city. I go for a half hour without stopping, twisting through all the dark parts and picking up speed with every turn. My pockets are filled with Russian coins and I begin throwing them in the air, making it rain dull rubles for several yards.

This is how long a second lasts.

Look At How Fast I Can Go Nowhere At All

As if I were the pin in the hands of a clock, time has moved around me. I'm the last one left. I speak to the wives now, maybe a dozen of them in the whole country, driving for hours at a time just to put them at ease. The first thing they always say is some remark about how well I've stayed put together, how lucky I am to have mobility at my age. Like me, they were barely twenty years old when the *USS Indianapolis* sank and stopped everything, became the moment that defined what happened before it, the reason nothing happened after it. I don't tell the story and they don't ask me to, which is good, because I tell it coldly, as pure fact, straight numbers. There's twelve: the number of minutes it took the ship to sink. There's one thousand, one hundred and ninety-six: the number of men on the boat. There's three hundred and sixteen: the number of men who managed to survive four days attached to a handful of lifeboats, fending off shark attacks, living without food or water. I mostly just listen. They tell me about their husbands. None of them have let it go. I get lonesome marriage proposals from a wife in Lawrence, Kansas, a wife in Ybor City, Florida. The one in Oklahoma City speaks at me in feverish, rabid French. Two rest home attendants have to come in and calm her down. One tries to get her to breathe in a regular pattern while the other holds her hand and rubs gently between her shoulder blades. One time, as I'm leaving, I'm told that she's never happier than after meeting with me, but the excitement puts too much strain on her heart. I'm not invited back, and I drive on to Cheyenne and Philipsburg and San Diego. I drive to July 30th, 1945 and everything I drink along the way smacks of saltwater.

The King

Montoya will teach you how to box. Brooks will teach you how to kill. When I started, I started with Montoya, watching videos, learning steps. It became imperative that I seek out the rhythms. Montoya told me I hit hard enough already, but I need to find the balance of competition. I thought I'd be clever and ask him how delicate this supposed balance is.

"It's a balance," he said. "If it isn't delicate, you're just some *pendejo* standing there with padded mittens on."

He would yell at me, quiz me as I was doing shadow-rounds with the other mentees. "What is balance?"

Jab. "Balance is." Block. Block. "The absolute center between control and chaos."

"Good. Why is it important?"

Block. Hook. Block. "To cultivate virtue and grace and through those." Jab. Block. "Back to balance."

"Right, right. And what does that all mean?"

Right cross.

Ten count.

"Don't fuck with me."

I WON FIGHTS, MOVED UP THE CIRCUIT, FOUGHT FOR TITLES. I never won any. I began to lose fights and move back down the circuit. I blamed Montoya and his ideas. I decided I needed more time in the ring, so I went to a different gym one day, alone, to take on anyone who was looking to spar a bit. I beat three men easily, tough guys who wouldn't have lasted long in a bar fight, let alone in the ring. I had hardly broken a sweat, so I threw shadow punches in the ring after everyone left.

I heard a voice from the entranceway of the room say, "I never seen someone punch like that. There's no way that greasy spic taught you that."

I stopped and turned around, half ready to defend Montoya and half just looking for any sort of a fight.

"I see the way you're looking at me, kid," the voice said. "But I'm not stepping in that ring. Not with you or anyone else. Montoya made you a decent fighter, but you wouldn't even last a minute going up against a pile of my soft shit."

I bounced on my toes a bit to keep the blood flowing, but before I could respond, Brooks said, "So, kid, don't fucking look at me that way."

I climbed out of the ring and stood in front of him, noses an inch apart. He was surprisingly tall. "If it's your job as a boxer," he said, "to win the fight, then that means it's your job to hurt, to cause pain. You can get in my face all you want and you can even keep listening to that wetback Montoya, but right now, I can tell you don't have the nuts to do your goddamn job. If I'm wrong, then do it."

It was just me and Brooks. When I hadn't taken a swing after about a half minute, Brooks moved so close our noses touched and, without lowering his voice, said, "So. Kid. Don't fucking look at me that way."

I began training with Brooks the next day. He never

stipulated that I had to stop training with Montoya, but I never went back, never even called to tell him I was through.

HE ALREADY TOLD ME I HAD THE BEST RAW PUNCHES HE HAD ever seen, but Brooks said that Montoya had cluttered me up with jargon to make me do whatever he wanted.

So I spent most of my time training with ropes around my waist and hands: if I wanted to be a puppet, Brooks would treat me like one.

We went back to the same gym I had beaten the three chumps at. Brooks laid out the open challenge for anyone to step into the ring with me, but word had gotten around about my training, my past. And underground, Brooks' reputation outweighed even Montoya's.

Brooks had anticipated this, so he offered me up tied in the ropes. I would have to be smarter and faster than not only the man I was fighting, but Brooks as well. When I went to throw a punch, Brooks would jerk my hand in the other direction. If I was trying to move into position quickly, he would tug the rope around my waist to the side and throw me off. It was dangerous, nonsensical the way he pulled me around the ring. I lost every fight.

"I don't know about this, Brooks," I told him at the end of the day.

"You're goddamn right you don't. Take that shit off and get back in there."

I took off the ropes. The men who stepped up lasted ten seconds.

A FEW WEEKS INTO MY TRAINING, MONTOYA SHOWED UP WITH

a few of his students. I recognized the one walking next to Montoya, the star pupil behind me. He was a mountainous, 290-pound Hispanic kid who had been making a name for himself in the circuit. I had fought him only once before leaving, but I remember him throwing clunky haymakers that, if aimed correctly, could keep the regional dentistry business thriving for years. I knew by the way his feet rolled on the ground, the way his arms hung by his sides, that his unwieldiness was gone. Manny Guererra. The Marauder.

The history between Brooks and Montoya became apparent almost immediately. They approached each other slowly. As if in a film, Marauder and I stood behind our respective mentors and stared stone-faced into one another as they bickered over everything, not just the difference in their styles, but money that was owed from one to the other in the 1970s, girlfriends who had defected from Brooks to Montoya and then back and then back and then back.

Men who had been jumping rope and sparring stopped to listen. As everyone began to anticipate the showdown between Marauder and me, I broke my stare. I closed my eyes and thought of the things they had taught me separately and, now, together, their breaths hot and vitriolic, mixing in one another's faces.

I WON'T SAY WHO WON THE FIGHT. I WON'T EVEN SAY IF IT actually happened. I will say that I stopped training with both men and, years later, fought Marauder in his last match. He died in the ring of a massive heart attack. I was past my prime, and a hardness in me peeled away as he fell. When his gloves dropped and he began to topple, I did not swing, did not even think of it.

When the autopsy results came back, we found out that Marauder's heart was the size of a normal man's head. His lungs were like sleeping bags. How all that viscera fit into one man, nobody could understand. I went to the funeral and saw Montoya and Brooks for the first time since the incident at the gym years prior. I began training by myself after that day at the gym, and whether or not Marauder had switched from Montoya to Brooks and back I don't know. He was alone when I fought him, on top of the world and nobody even close to him. I would have lost the bout had it gone another two rounds.

I paid my respects and walked back to my car. As I sat down, Montoya knocked on my driver's side window. A moment later, Brooks knocked on my passenger side window. They were ignoring each other and I was ignoring them. For some reason, I thought of when I was a young kid, maybe four or five, and I heard that Elvis had died. Something important I knew nothing about was gone and never coming back.

PLOTS

Bobby Fischer and I were both thirteen in 1956. The day he beat Donald Byrne in the "game of the century," my mother bought me a chess board. She became obsessed with it, staying up late into the night to read books on strategy and history. She saw potential in it, both for me and for America, and she was half right. Bobby went on to unseat the Soviet Union from their dominance in chess before I could.

I never amounted to much on the board – too much emphasis on spatial patterns that I couldn't see, let alone memorize. Still, my mother's focus was unstoppable. We played each other thousands of times, sitting at a card table in the living room with the television on mute and a record on the turntable. When *Pet Sounds* came out, she played it every night for the next six years while we sat there and moved pieces on the board, endlessly and, for me, aimlessly. I spent my teens and twenties absorbing brass instruments and surf guitar and not much else. My mother drank black Russians as if that was in itself a form of domination. She was sending the entire country down her throat. She learned how to speak Russian, and she would taunt me as we played. Her grin was wicked, her face twisted, Mona Lisa with an aneurysm.

After Bobby beat Boris Spassky for the World

Championship in 1972, my mother abandoned hope for my chess career. The empire had fallen and, with America safe, she was content enough to die a few years later. I tried playing competitively for a while in New York. I was a joke even on the amateur circuit, and the city scared me. Men in pinstripe suits smoked as a prime function of breathing and used the smoldering cherry at the tip of their fat cigars to light the cigarettes of the burlesque dancers that sat on their laps. Their breath was thick like blood and they laughed through sore throats.

I hopped a train headed home and when I got there I stayed. I took a maintenance and custodial job at a zoo about an hour away from my house. On my lunch breaks I'd play chess with the other workers and usually lose. I met up with one of the girls who worked in the bird conservatory. She beat me every day for a week. At the end of our last game she said, "Why didn't you move your king's bishop sooner? You would have had me." I told her I didn't know. "You're not picking this up too fast, are you?" she said and punched me lightly in the arm. When I walked her back to her station, I noticed that she had a faint smell of sweat and grain about her. She was twenty that summer and I was creeping through my mid-thirties. Bobby himself had turned into a memory after failing to defend his title in 1975.

I had only been in the conservatory at night to clean, with minimal lighting to see the floors. I had never been in the cages, but I could hear the birds. They fluttered and called to one another. Their sounds were cacophonous but smooth. We reached the cages and I saw no colors, only the black of the birds, perched and ready to circle.

WIDE RIGHT GAME

There's an apartment building I used to steal from when I was old enough to know better but young enough to be forgiven. The people who lived there were described as lower middle class, but bullshit aside they were poor people who owned a few small things like CD players and deep fryers. Often enough they hoarded comic books and sports memorabilia that they refused to part with. Mostly they just buried all their stuff in a pile somewhere and forgot about it.

In addition to the noises of the structure itself — broken gutters clattering against the side of the building, every hinge a rusty, symphonic mess — everyone drank and slept heavily. I'd sneak in during the middle of the night through the fire escape and leave through the front door with stuff to pawn a few towns over. I sold a six-pack of Billy Beer for $35, a 1970's Aerosmith tour shirt for $50.

One night I crawled through the window of someone's apartment at three in the morning and saw a man on the couch, an old football game on the television. I was startled at first, but he was definitely out, bottle of whiskey still in his hand and a glass of something spilled and pooled into a ballooned-out shape on the rug. I looked back at the television. Bills vs. Giants. Super Bowl XXV. The game was in its final moments: the Bills are down by one and placekicker Scott Norwood needs to make the 47-yard field goal with eight seconds left. He fucks it. The announcer yells *No good! Wide right!* The Giants are jumping up and down into each other's arms, lifting Bill Parcells onto their shoulders and walking the sidelines. MVP Ottis Anderson grabs a mini American flag and dedicates the game to the Gulf War troops. The deep voiceover calls it the Wide Right Game. Scott Norwood walks off the field with his head up.

I began rooting through the man's possessions and not finding much. His apartment was a two bedroom, but one room was empty except bottles of booze and beer, some of them half full with a film congealing on top, dead gnats stuck to it. I found nothing in there. In the room with a bed, there was a dresser that was empty, all the clothes in piles on the floor, almost sorted and leaking into one another like watercolors. His white shirts turned into his navy pants turned into his underwear and socks. I went back to the kitchen, and though I was usually nimble, quick and sharp with my hands, the bottom fell out of a box I lifted, scattering metal spatulas and beaters into a huddle and then out, like a wave.

When I looked into the living room, the man was still on the couch, unmoved, the current-day in-studio announce team talking about Scott Norwood's career paralleling the decline and restructuring of the city of Buffalo itself. I had never seen a dead man up close before. His skin was yellowed and thin except around his nose and eyes where capillaries had burst like a rash.

I began cleaning his apartment, arranging his magazines and video tapes. I threw away the dirty ones. I moved back to his room and put the laundry into garbage bags to be cleaned and folded later. I went through his fridge and cupboards and threw out the junk food. I swept the floor, dusted his end-tables and television. In the spare bedroom I began placing the bottles into bags of their own, two at a time, not spilling or making a sound.

I grabbed a bowl and filled it with warm water and soap and began cleaning him. I used a bath towel and went all over his body, lifting up his belly and wiping off a moist, sun-colored layer of filth the consistency of paste. I put him in a fresh change of clothes and threw the stained shorts and shirt he was wearing into the garbage before twisting the top of the garbage itself and setting it by the front door. There were dozens of bags of trash. I took all the remaining alcohol in the house and dumped it down the sink, bottles of cheap Mr. Boston's gin and vodka, shitty light beer from gas stations and convenience marts.

I went back into his room again to make his bed and saw a Polaroid of two women tucked into the mirror of the dresser. On the bottom it said *Nancy and Jacqueline* and a recent date, only the previous summer. Nancy was motioning toward the camera, trying to shake away whoever was taking the picture, but Jacqueline was beautiful, glowing sheepishly and looking to be my age, though incapable of thievery and probably on track to graduate high school. I grabbed the picture and shoved it too hard, too fast into my back pocket and crinkled it along the V-shaped bottom.

JACQUELINE DOESN'T ASK ME ABOUT HER FATHER OFTEN, AND I don't press my luck with it, either. I don't look for sympathy or try to weasel my way out of an argument by saying *It's like your father told me once*. I told her when I met her—the pretty Irish girl with bad eyes squinting back and forth between the preacher and the urn—that I had been helping her father get back on track for the past few months before he died. He was almost there, almost ready to call her and show him what he had accomplished.

We're watching television one day and she's flipping through the channels. The kids are sleeping and the sound's down low. She pauses on a sports channel for a second and I recognize it, Bills vs. Giants, Super Bowl XXV. I reach out my hand like I'm warning a car to a halt. I say, *It's the game* and then I stop. She flips back to it and then squints at me a bit, still pretty, still going blind. We finish watching until the end and she comments on poor Scott Norwood. I watch the replay closer this time. From one camera angle, the distance is long and painful. From another, the laces on the ball are clearly facing Norwood. He didn't have a chance. I think of Jacqueline's father, bloated and glorious.

When There Is No Road

Wednesday night at the Pine Box Social Club is karaoke with a live band. Thursday night is fight night. Hank's vision flashes sometimes, but he still goes to both. He's forty-six and too old for the circuit. His voice and his face go together well.

The locals know him. He sings "Street Fighting Man" and "Saturday Night's Alright For Fighting." Anyone who wins a fight gets an open tab for a week. If Hank doesn't win, people buy him drinks. The night pushes back and the songs get slower, "Fearless Heart" by Steve Earle and "Atlantic City" by Springsteen. The band has been around too long, as if they were found playing on the road one day and a bar was built around them.

HANK'S BEEN WORRIED ABOUT THE FLASHES MORE AND MORE lately. About a year ago some trucker from Maine was passing through for the night and decided to get in on the fights. He loaded his glove with some of the smooth, flat stones from the rock bed out front and when he landed a punch on Hank a minute into the first round, it only took one more a second later to end it.

The locals ran him out, nearly burned down his rig after he crawled into it and started it up, and when Hank came to, the flashes were worse. Instead of the light receding and then building back up a moment later, like an old television turned off and then back on quickly, the flashes came in short bursts of varying strengths, like sheets of rain.

SOME THURSDAY NIGHTS, AFTER ALL THE FIGHTS ARE DONE, Hank will sit in his car just listening to the radio. There are times when he won't leave the parking lot until the next morning. His car will idle all night and the owner will have to come out and give him a jump.

No station comes in clear enough anymore. Every rhythm section sounds like it's in the breeze. Every song is a whisper, a secret.

BOXERS HIT HARDER IN AUTUMN. NOBODY'S PROVED IT OR even done a study on it, but watching Hank punch his way through November is different than watching him punch his way through April or July. There's no season to the sport, but there is the inverse: here is a thing you cannot stop.

THERE ARE BETTER SINGERS IN THE WORLD THAN HANK. There's even a better singer in the Pine Box Social Club on the live karaoke nights, and it's a safe bet that there's a better singer in every bar in every town. "You don't need a good voice if you've got a good right hook," Hank said once. He shrugged and some people in the bar began talking simple philosophy—each of our unique gifts. They had all seen Hank's right hook and decided that it wasn't developed so much as it was bestowed upon him.

For the first time in years, Hank didn't show up to fight night. It was a few weeks ago and people were calling his house, trying to find him. Jim Mikinez was declared the most sober and put in charge of driving to Hank's house to see if he was okay. The bartender gave him a bottle of Old Style for the drive.

Jim was back about an hour later. "Damnedest thing," he said. "I go over to Hank's place and he's sitting in his car in his driveway, like he does here some nights, blasting his stereo."

People did think it was the damnedest thing, and when Hank came back the next week, nobody mentioned it to him. Jim left a part out, though, in his telling of the story. It was the part that scared him, about how Hank had the windows down and the car in a full idle, revving the pedal along to the song. The car would rock a bit, and Jim knew it was in drive, not park. Hank's foot was on both the gas and the brake. Jim watched until he couldn't take it anymore, the thought of Hank letting go of either pedal, the motion that would follow.

It's Been Far Too Long Since You Woke Up In Someone Else's Shoes

Back in high school you had a girl and a band and you thought both of them would last forever. That was ten years ago. Things have a funny way of swinging around in wide arcs. Sometimes it's like a wave and sometimes it's like a haymaker. No matter what, in the morning you're breathing heavy and nursing a headache.

But, things. And the way they swing around. Everyone's back: you, the girl, the band. *One night only* people keep saying. You're all creeping up on thirty and planning a kegger on a farm where everything is borrowed except time and money, which isn't to say anyone there will have much of either.

The guitarist set it all up. He tried to kill himself five or six years ago. You had no idea until you picked him up and he gave you convoluted directions to the farm so he could talk awhile.

"I'm trying to figure out what I owe," he said, clicking the button for the power window down and letting it go, then doing it again.

"I've got some extra cash if it's –"

"Never mind."

The girl is the first one you see, of course. It's worse than a high school reunion, the way you feel obligated to present the high points of your life. You have no job and the most important person in your life is your mother, who you drive home to see once a week. She makes you lunch and gives you your laundry back, clean and folded and put into the basket you dropped off the week before. Instead of saying any of that, you pretend to barely remember the girl.

More than once during your conversation you take a big drag off a cigarette and don't respond to whatever it is she's asked you, as if your mouth were full of food instead of smoke. Minutes later, the only thing you can recall her saying is that she's single. Too many things are not different, not the same. You decide not to have sex with her if the opportunity arises. Then you change your mind. Then you start drinking.

A few hours later, you play. The songs are easy and you play them well, but it's routine. You thought you were saying something about rock and roll when you played those songs a decade ago. You know it isn't rock and roll that's changed, but you refuse to believe it's you.

Afterwards, someone you sometimes used to talk to comes up to you and says *you have to see this*. You're drunk and it's a female, so you care. She's holding a copy of the CD you gave her years back, just some demos recorded in the garage and burned to a blank disc. You don't even have one anymore. She shows you the top so you can see the singer's fancy, elongated letters spelling out the name of the band and the names of the songs. Then she turns it over and you both stand there for a second, your face stretched awkwardly in the reflection from the disc.

It's late.

You find the girl in bed, alone. She's awake and you both start revealing things about yourselves so fast that you're speaking almost simultaneously. She talks mostly about how she feels she'll end up alone, and how it's kind of your fault. You talk about how you feel as if you're underappreciated, how everything you do comes out skewed compared to how it sounded when it was just something in your head.

This is where you forget what happened. You remember feeling sick and going to get another drink. Someone poured you a shot. Tequila. You wake up in the morning hoping you went back to the bedroom with the girl. Because you know the right things were not done, you hope they were at least said.

The guitarist wakes you up last after you pass out again. Everyone else is gone and he needs a ride back into town. You stand up and feel like the bottom fell out of your stomach and kept going. When you look down, you see that you're wearing a pair of blue Reeboks. You bounce up onto your toes and then back down. Not yours, but they fit well.

The guitarist looks at you for a moment, then says, "Are you ready to go?"

"Man, they really fucked this place up," you say, still looking at the shoes.

"Yeah."

You want to shake his hand, give him a hug.

Something.

Monsters:
A Series of Non-Chronological Vignettes

College Apartment #3, December 21, 1999

I just started a KISS tribute band with my friends. We're going to play our first show on Valentine's Day: A Kiss with KISS. My car is filled with their discs and I listen to them everywhere I go, trying to revisit the songs and learn them through repetition. The first one I break scraping off my windshield is *Psycho Circus*, which I won't necessarily miss. There goes *Lick It Up*. *Animalize* is shattered, flakes of the label mixing in with the snow on my gloves. It finally comes down to which disc of *Alive!* will be sacrificed. I decide that the girl will stay, she and I and Jesus Christ to save our issues for later.

House-sitting, July 5-13, 2000

WE KISS FOR TWENTY MINUTES. NOT A MAKE-OUT SESSION, BUT a kiss, our lips pressed together and held, as if in an embrace.

When we finally pull back from each other, I say, "I could live here."

"You do live here."

31

We spend most of our time unclothed and barely touching, flinching at the slam of a car door or ring of a phone not because of our nakedness, but because of our company. Of all the things we do in secret, the most enjoyable is the idyllic banalities of domesticity: she in a long dress trying to figure out how to make chicken cacciatore and me putting together a bookshelf without any instructions, stripping screws until we laugh and collapse into the couch, a half-built monstrosity on the floor next to us.

The Only Coffee Shop In Town, September 3, 1999

AFTER RUNNING IT BY HER BIBLE STUDY GROUP FOR A COUPLE months, she decided to break off her engagement to her boyfriend of six years.

"He doesn't believe in the Lord," she tells me, drinking cheap tea and listening to talk radio.

I know him, and I like what little I know about him, his sense of humor and intelligence. "Charming guy, though, from what I can tell."

"Right, of course." She blows over the top of her tea. "When I first met him he charmed my pants—"

"Loose, right?" I'm unafraid of how I feel, like having a crush on a lesbian or a supermodel. "He charmed your pants loose, but not off."

"Right," she says, blushing. "Of course."

Uh-O, April 18, 2000

IN THE AMUSING WAY IN WHICH PEOPLE SET UP THEIR OWN personal barriers when defining right and wrong, she won't allow me to bring her to orgasm.

Supermarket Sweep, November 20, 2000

USING THE VERNACULAR OF FATHERS ON SITCOMS, IT'S possible to get enough guys on third base and still get a couple runs. So it's not the absence of sex. It's the question of how much longer things can be sustained without having to come to terms with the nature of the relationship, how much longer her upstanding reputation as a good child of the Lord will be more important than the facts of the situation as it exists.

I go, "How will we ever go about moving in together? What if we want to get married? Will it have to be by a justice of the peace in a remote town in Montana? Will our kids be homeschooled and sleep at the houses of actors we pay to pretend to be their parents?"

She starts crying, softly but immediately. She puts back all the items she was going to buy to make spaghetti, but I buy a Whatchamacallit. She doesn't go to the car and wait, just stands next to me trying not to make a scene. I want to feel bad, but instead I drop her off at her apartment and then go to mine by myself. Just like that, I know we won't speak anymore, and like everything else that makes easy sense coming together, I feel as if I had been bracing myself for such a schism from the moment I snapped that first KISS disc against the ice on my windshield: *Right. Of course.*

Monsters, December 29, 1999

SHE SAYS SHE HASN'T BEEN DANCING IN YEARS, SINCE HIGH school when her ex-fiancé and her went to prom. Within an hour my car is stuck in a cornfield. I was trying to find the perfect spot, and when I couldn't maneuver the car out of the spot I was in, I looked around and saw that the perfect spot had, in a way, found us.

She still has no idea what we're doing, but she doesn't press the issue. I leave the car running and turn on the high-beams. I get out and she follows suit. I take her hand about twenty feet in front of the car and for two hours, three hours, we dance until the snow beneath us is packed solid and our cheeks are numb. Our shadows stretch off to our sides like monsters. She cranes her neck up to touch our foreheads together and the breath between the kiss is almost more important than the kiss itself.

Rust

Neil was the strongest guy I knew, which was good, because it meant I didn't have to be. There were plenty of other reasons to like him, but his strength was the thing everyone commented on. Even me, and I had known him since primary school, since the first time I saw him take a pencil, grip it with his teeth like a Spanish woman with a rose in her mouth, and then break it with his tongue.

That's what I mean by strong: literal, physical power. Not that he wasn't the other kind, too, the kind where he scared the world off him enough to make sure he moved with a kindly grace—because he was—but it was always just easier to get caught up in the fanfare of someone pushing a Volkswagen up an incline.

I've got twenty-four-inch biceps. That's pretty big. We're talking Hulk Hogan big. Neil and I were great together at parties, doing the classic strongman pose with a woman sitting on each arm as we flexed, the four of them looking like little girls on their first horse ride. The thing about Neil, though, is that he wasn't big, and that threw people. I don't just mean he wasn't big compared to me. I mean that he wasn't big. I've got an eight-inch wrist and Neil looked like an accountant and I never beat him in arm wrestling.

The other thing about Neil is that he had the sort of problems that strength can't fix. He self-destructed with women and had no skills that he was proud of, nothing that made him feel he was making anything better than how he found it. "Come into a bad situation and make it good. That's what men do, right?" he said to me one night down in the rock quarry behind his folks' place.

"I guess. Shit, I don't know," I told him.

We were especially restless that summer, both of us twenty and home from college for those few hot months, and to blow off steam we'd pick up the biggest rocks we could find in the quarry and see who could toss them the farthest.

Neil picked up a rock and balanced it on his shoulder. "Don't you think that's the real measure of a man? To buff out as much rust as he can before he's gone?"

"I don't think you buff rust out."

"Well," Neil paused and sent the rock flying through the air. "Count it off."

I walked heel-to-toe from where Neil was standing to where the rock landed. Seventeen feet. When I turned around to tell him, he was gone.

"Neil, come on down here you sonofabitch."

"I can see just fine," he yelled back. He was up on the ledge off to the side of me, lying on his back with his head hanging over the side. "Go on, toss already."

I wondered how he got up there so fast. I felt as if when Neil laid his head back over that ledge, that he turned the whole world upside down, like he was right-side-up and it was everything else, including me, that flipped.

When he died a few years later—some freak car accident that was as plain as any other bad news until it happened to me—I went to the funeral late. Not many people were left there and I got to walk right up to the casket. I remember thinking that it wasn't a very big box. How the hell did Neil fit in there? How'd it take me until then to finally understand his strength? Nobody was looking, so I went over to the bottom corner of the casket and stuck my hand under the edge. Jesus, the things I've lifted. Boat engines, one in each hand. Old console record players. Fifty-five gallon drums of peanut oil. But I'll be goddamned if that box moved an inch, a centimeter, not space enough for the thinnest light to sneak beneath it.

The Vikings

Think of every dollar you'll ever make in your entire life. That's how much money Wade and Ricky spend a year on cigarettes and pills. The total sum of their worth doesn't go up or down in any noticeable amount, it just fluctuates throughout the stock market like so many gallons of water in an ocean. My worth is countable. Theirs isn't even tangible.

My job is to watch them and make sure they don't die. The pay is mostly incentive based: for every day I work for Wade and Ricky and they don't die, they'll put five hundred dollars into a savings account.

"Think about it," Wade said after he hired me for the personal assistant position I was expecting to do. "If everything goes smooth for six years, you'll be a millionaire."

Ricky set a revolver on my lap and put his hand on my shoulder. "Just don't cash out early." Nobody said anything. After a few moments, he reached down and picked the revolver back up, tucking it back into his pants.

They paid me to worry. I watched them take pills to wake and then hours later take pills to fall asleep. They had a pill for every action and its opposite: to get an erection, to make it go down, to feel better, to feel worse.

I've been with them two years. Some nights I fall

asleep thinking about the $300,000 I've already made, sitting there waiting for me. Some nights I fall asleep thinking about Ricky's gun, warm and heavy on my thighs. Some nights I don't fall asleep.

WADE AND RICKY EACH TOOK A HANDFUL OF PILLS THIS morning. Now we're in Switzerland.

The two of them have become increasingly concerned about their mortality, their place in history. "Lots of guys have lots of dough," Wade told me on the jet. "It doesn't make us special." He and Ricky tried explaining their idea to me, something about a world record and a mobile home. I couldn't understand it. Their sentences mashed together, with one finishing the other's and while that person then continued on from a different but just as seemingly logical point, creating an odd web of parallel universe-styled conversations.

I checked their pulses, their blood pressures.

THE ROPE HOLDING THE HOUSEBOAT BURNED AWAY TO nothing. I jumped out onto the dock and the boat floated slowly off with the ebb of the water. We felt like Vikings, though we had lost nothing in the fire, sent no fallen comrade away.

We had gone over to the docks to talk to someone about mobile homes. The first three were empty. Ricky kicked the door in on the last one. He wrote out a check for a new door as we looked for a phone book. There were playing cards everywhere, some set up in the middle of a game, but mostly just dozens of decks stacked in corners and singles scattered on flat surfaces. In one of the cupboards, I found a tiny roulette wheel. I spun it and it was so smooth that it went around for almost a half a minute. I bet it all on red.

Ricky found a flare gun and shot it off. The bed caught on fire. Within a minute, the roof lit up. By then I had corralled them toward the door and out of it. "Wait here and write a check," I said. I ripped the door off what little bit of hinge remained and then ran back inside. I started throwing piles of anything that wasn't a bunch of goddamn playing cards out onto the dock, hoping I was saving irreplaceable items, heirlooms and school pictures from years ago. I planned on dropping the check and the things I could save off at a neighboring boat. When the smoke was getting too bad to breathe, I grabbed the pictures off the walls and from the countertops.

I looked at the roulette wheel. The ball was seated firmly in a red divot. "Lies," I said. I jumped onto the dock and watched the smoke rising into the sky. It moved off in wisps, so many different shades and hues. The colors of a lifetime.

WE'RE AT A HOTEL NOW. WADE AND RICKY HAVE GIVEN UP the idea of the mobile home and taken more pills, another fistful each. At the front desk, they ask for more mattresses and pillows to be brought to the suite. Money takes care of the inconvenience. They line the walls with the mattresses. They order more lamps to the room and cover the bulbs with coffee filters they've colored with a red marker. The room looks like a photographer's darkroom.

They invent their wrestling names and take turns slingshotting each other into the mattresses, bouncing off and then slamming one another onto the pillows on the floor. Ricky nails a powerslam, Wade hits a back body drop. I'm not amused, have, in fact, been unamused by these two for so long that I don't remember what it's like to be entertained.

They're slowing down. Wade botches a simple hip toss and they both collapse. I check their pulses. Normal, all things considered. With no place to lie down, I sit in one of the large chairs in the room and put the footrest out. I lean the chair back and recline until I'm almost flat. Wade and Ricky are still breathing deeply into the pillows. I'm not tired. Part of my life is trapped in a bank account, part of my life is stuffed full of a few thousand milligrams of Xedafidamin and passed out on the ground. If I close my eyes, it's all still there. It's quiet for minutes. Then, in an even voice, I hear Ricky ask me if I remember that time, years ago, he says, when we burned down that boat.

"No," I say. "Tell me about it."

Signal

I'm watching home videos from other people's lives. I buy them in stacks at Goodwill outlets and thrift stores for fifty cents each, a dollar at most. It's important that these people aren't me and aren't people I know, so I drive for miles sometimes to find the old videos of strangers. I watch Troy's first day of school. I watch Tim and Judy's wedding. I watch fifth-grade band concerts, over and over again.

Tonight I watch Thanksgiving 1991. The tape starts with a close-up of a turkey and pans out to show the stuffing, the cranberries, the gravy and bread and mashed potatoes. The chairs and room are empty. The voice behind the camera is joyous in its clarity. The narrator sets the camera on the counter and walks in front of it to continue talking, resting his hands on the backs of chairs and making small talk about high school jazz combos and imported cigars and sold-out plays. The conversation is there but the guests are not. The narrator is wearing a blue pinstripe blazer and khaki pants and his hair is combed neatly to the front, graying slightly. He lifts a glass and stands quietly at the head of the table.

I propose a toast. Here. To this.

The man sits down and dips a piece of bread into the

gravy. He eats several plates of food and then leaves the room without shutting off the video camera. The radio plays in the background for the rest of the tape. The songs are indecipherable. Everything has been thinned from amp to album, album to radio, radio to camera, camera to television, television to ears. A signal so distant, its whimpers are pinpricks.

--:--

The year she thought she saw David Lee Roth at a Mets game, she married the first man who didn't care when she told him about it. He was a marine-biologist and she baked cakes, so their conversations were about people, not things. Nine years later they were looking over the railing of a boat going from New York to the British Isles when he said, "Subsurface currents are formed by one mass of water meeting another mass of water that is of similar composition but inverted in its essence. In this sense, it is like making fog or arch enemies."

Then he jumped.

I'M SUMMARIZING. WHEN WE TELL STORIES, WE TELL JUST enough of them to make them real.

One would think the girl and the water would be real enough on their own. But we all have our own girls, our own water to contend with.

This might do it: the night he jumped, she laid herself on his bed and became him for the night, listing off fabricated information about the oceans with all the conviction of gravity behind her.

TOO OFTEN, A MAN IS DEFINED BY WHAT HE SAYS AND DOES and a woman is defined by her reaction. It's justified by sympathy—he did jump into an ocean, after all—and grief—her husband did jump into an ocean, after all. Grief especially does strange things to people, which is why it's the only word needed when talking to a friend about a mutual friend's terrible new haircut.

It's used in stories in a removed manner. The character's grief is that of the writer, is that of the reader. That distance makes everyone seem further away and, thus, more important. When the story is told, it's possible to see for miles the complexities that belong to both of us, scattered between our feet in a line straighter than the surface of still water.

If I say that the only thing the man did as he was drowning was remove his wedding ring and swallow it, why is your life the one that's different?

HAUNT

June was dead like me. Like all of us in the city. She wasn't my wife, but we took each other on in that same way, making the needs of the other equal to our own. We spent our time living like the living as much as we could, talking about people around the city and, on the occasions it happened, sharing memories we had from when we were alive. One day June came up to me and told me that she remembers what it was like to breathe out slowly over ice cream on a hot day and watch the steam rise in a puff up into the air.

The city is mostly tendrils, thick green spines wrapping up everything until the tendrils themselves are everything. They tangle together at random and spill further beyond any point that any of us have journeyed. The tendrils were the first thing I saw when I arrived here. They're the first thing everyone saw when they arrived here. We all had the same experience, wandering into the city and being enamored with them, what they could possibly be attached to if not themselves and the way they had swallowed everything in their way when climbing toward the sun. Later on we all joked about how caught up on them we were and how important it seemed until we realized that we were dead.

There were about a hundred people in the city when I

showed up. I knew it couldn't be a place for everyone who had died. There just weren't enough people. Of the ones who were there, a few of us had been there for a long time. Though the sky was constantly at dusk and no clocks existed, the concept of time wasn't completely lost. We tried to gauge time by who had come and gone during our time in the city. Aside from Maddox, June and I had been there the longest, with me showing up right after her and meeting her almost immediately. I arrived in front of her as if appealing to an empress. Maddox was a handsome seventeen or eighteen year old who looked vaguely Spanish, and he could recall when everyone had come into the city, what it was like when he saw them for the first time.

"Man, when you came in, I don't think I've laughed that hard since I got here," he said to me once. "You just wandered around for awhile, checking out the tendrils, and then you finally walked up to June and said, 'Why don't I want a sandwich?'"

He wasn't a greeter—nobody had a job, even one like that—but nobody could show up and go too long without running into everyone. It was like that every day. We all did the same things in the same places, trying to figure out whether we were going to end up here forever or if we needed to die a little more. Some of us got out, usually the ones who weren't there for too long to begin with— though a girl named Jeanne was there almost as long as anyone when she just vanished one day, dissipated into a fuzzy gray and then into nothing.

Everyone in the city had a memory full of holes, the thoughts laid out like a puzzle with all the wrong pieces missing. So we—Maddox, June, and I—started writing them down almost as a hobby, if such a thing could exist.

We wrote down every detail about every person and tried to find the common ground between us all. If we couldn't leave, we at least wanted to figure out why we were there.

To be honest, there wasn't much we had figured out. We didn't know why any of it happened. The appearances. The disappearances. We collected facts numbering in the tens of thousands. It still made no sense. Maddox thought it was because we had something to do somewhere else, that being stuck in the city wasn't what we were supposed to be doing, and when we were ready to move on, we moved on. I was always glad when people disappeared. It meant that the city wasn't the end.

Once, June told me that she thought I was only partly right. "The city's just one of many ends," she said. It was odd of her to say. She never brought up the disappearances. But then I noticed her figure, how wispy she was becoming. We sat down on the floor of the city and didn't speak. She turned into different shades of dirty milk, becoming more and more transparent, and I wondered how many times we'd have to lose what we had, how many ends we'd have to come to.

After I Threw the Ball At Thomas Hernandez and Before It Killed Him

I can't say it was an accident, but in my defense I can say that the last time I encountered Thomas Hernandez he stole home from me twice: once during the game and once after it. When he tried it again this time, he got caught in a pickle. Anne was in the stands, only slightly amused by the Mexican minor leagues but completely unable to escape the men who play in it. She still flew down for the occasional game, but to see Hernandez instead of me. When I started closing the gap between myself and the catcher, Hernandez pivoted between us and his helmet flew off. I saw Anne stand up for the first time ever at a game. Hernandez slid into home, and as the stitches rolled off the pads of my fingers I seemed to have all the time I wanted to justify it, to think about how everyone knows that my throws have been fast and sloppy as of late, how the coroner will place the pitch in the upper-eighties and everyone will rule it an accident while still thinking in the back of his head that I may have done it on purpose. They won't know that they're all right, that I had time to think about how I've earned my darkness and refused to believe that I have no brightness that needs suppressing, that I've thought about it all and decided that, yes, I deserve the best sleep that can be had by a man alone in bed.

Follow the Water

actoring in time spent blacked-out and lost, the full circuit takes a little over a week to do. I think the easiest way is by starting in Humboldt with Drano Dave. You'll spend the first four days there if you're lucky. If you're really lucky, you won't die from the cleaning solvents Dave cuts everything with and you won't kill yourself after three sleepless days of being talked at. The last I heard, his new thing is putting on two eye-patches he calls his "infinitesimal passion extrapolation glasses" and narrating the beat of your heart until his voice runs out, at which point he takes your hand and taps his words out in Morse code across your knuckles.

Whatever you do, don't let him follow you.

Wander down into the Lower West Side. There's a bunch of wop diners lined up on Oakley. One in the middle sells balloons and they don't watch the helium tanks. You can sit there all day and if you're still fucked up enough from your stay in Humboldt, you'll think talking like a chipmunk for the next seven or eight hours will be the best thing in the world. Every medium sized huff kills about 400 brain cells. Other than that, you can't really hurt yourself. Make sure the last huff you take is a big one. The helium replaces the oxygen and if you have no oxygen you pass out, preferably not on the bike trail.

Hit the Loop and follow the water. You'll find whatever you want, but I suggest holding out on the heavy stuff until you get to Lake View. There's a guy behind Wrigley Field named Shakedown. He's not hard to find. He's the sort of guy who looks like people call him Shakedown and he's the one with the formaldehyde. You can either bring your own smokes or buy some off him. Tell him you want to dip them yourself. This is how the conversation will go.

"Shakedown, I'm going to dip these myself, if that's cool."

"That's not cool, motherfucker."

"All right. That's fine." Feign putting your smokes back in the pack. "I'll just let Seven know you're being a dick."

Nobody knows who Seven is or if he's even real. We all assume he isn't. For a long time we all thought he was just some burnout named Steven who dropped the "t" and was always looking for an excuse to test his heels on Shakedown's head, but some sketchy drifter saw Shakedown flipping out one night, arguing with a chained-up bike he was taking commands from, which is when a handful of us figured out that we could probably start using Seven as a threat.

Anyway, you're only going to need two or three of the formaldehyde dips. Only take a couple puffs at a time and never smoke more than one a day. If you do, you'll probably end up seeing Seven, too. Nobody's going to make you stay, but you won't be moving much.

Avondale is the big Polish neighborhood, and since you'll probably only be able to pronounce the letters "o" and "w" your best bet is to go there next. Find Suzi. She doesn't have anything you need, and that'll feel nice, to have something someone else needs, to be wanted at least once. We called her Lines & Wines for years. If you've got a little bit of either you won't be able to get rid of her until it's gone. But long enough will be long enough. And she likes a challenge. At this point, the two of you fucking will probably look like a blind person with one hand trying to put a length of rope into a tube sock.

You should go south, cut the corners of Hermosa and Logan Square and end up right back in Humboldt. The trick is to not get caught by the circuit. One girl started and did it for months. We all called her Jill Doe, Jane's lesser-known sister. The only thing we know her for now is those months on the circuit. When we found Jill afterwards, we saw that she bit her tongue mostly off. Still, nobody slagged her. She did it for the same reasons we all did it in the first place. Once you learn manners and the golden rule and all that other stuff, your life isn't even into double digits and it's already over. The thing with the circuit is that it's always different. The drugs and the people and even each step, it's never the same one twice, and there isn't a person I know who wouldn't bite their tongue off to tell you about it.

A Few Thoughts On Bloodlines

I: Fambly Tree

My little brother's homework is to make a family tree. I'm kind of helping him and kind of not. All of our grandparents were dead before either of us was born, so we get stuck fairly early on in the process. I ask if I can take a look at what he's got and he hands me the big piece of yellow construction paper he's writing on. So far, he's drawn a stump with about a dozen branches jutting out from it, for me and mom and our aunts, uncles, and cousins. There's a branch on the ground labeled "dad." Above the stump he's written "Fambly Tree." He's in second grade and just learning about silent letters. I'm almost sure he knows how to spell "family" the right way. I hand him the paper back and say, "Mom's mom was named Pearl."

II: We Can Put a Man In a Television Studio in Lima, Ohio

THOUGH I HAD, FOR THE MOST PART, PRETTY MUCH GIVEN UP mentally, there was still the matter of dealing with the simultaneous hot and cold flashes, the pain in my arms and legs, the nauseating discharge from both ends of my body, and other physical problems. I had survived a week before deciding I would go to the hospital. I hadn't slept since making that decision, and once I got there things degenerated quickly between me and the doctor. She said I needed a kind of help she couldn't provide. I argued that, with all the advances in all the fields of stem cell research and DNA testing, she should have a way to fix me. "We can put a man on the moon," I started to say, but she cut me off and said, "Prove it."

III: Secretariat, the Fluke

THE RUNT OF THE LITTER NEVER SOLD. FOR YEARS MY FATHER had been using selective breeding to create the healthiest beagles and Labradors he could, but there was always the runt, always the unexpected. I'd go down to the barn and listen as he tried to pitch it to people when they came over to buy the bigger, healthier dogs. "I'd have better luck filling that cocksucker full of cement and selling him as a doorstop," he once said. He explained to me that the racehorse Secretariat was won in a losing coin toss, with Secretariat's half sister being the preferred horse. Upon Secretariat's death it was discovered that he had a twenty-two pound heart, almost two and a half times the size of a normal horse's heart. My father sat on the ground next to the dog pen and let the runt lick his hand and wrist and then upward, to the veins that burst from the base of his forearm in what I could only think of at the time as brilliance.

Focus

Every morning I go to the edge of the cliff near my house and throw something off. It's always something small, washers or bolts from the garage, an empty bottle from the recycling bin. If Neil and I go into town to eat the night before, I'll grab a spoon or a napkin ring from the table and take it with me to throw off the next morning.

We live on top of a mountain and the drop is huge, at least a couple hundred feet to any sort of bottom. When we first moved up here a couple years ago, I was still worried about a few of the wilder men before Neil, the ones who focused too hard. Eddie's one of them. After Eddie and I broke up, he followed me into the restaurant where I was eating alone, and before I could ask him to sit down he grabbed my steak knife. He didn't say anything, just started carving up his hands, driving the blade up his palm and then between his knuckles and then back around his wrist and up again. Eddie was smart, and he lived and he was still smart after that, but he just wanted the intangibles back he had given me—time, effort, etc— and because that was impossible, he did what he did.

Jonah was another. I saw him on the street one day when I was walking to get a paper and he followed me home. Not maliciously, but right behind me, talking about how two people in love are broken and then rebuilt as a single unit. I was polite until I reached my house, at which point I figured the only thing I could do was go inside and lock the door. When he realized I wasn't going to let him in, he started crawling on his knees back and forth, up and down the gravel walk-up to my front door. He was shouting about how he'd do it until he ground his legs to nubs. He did it for a half hour and his pants were torn, his knees bloody. I finally broke down and invited him inside just for long enough to get his knees bandaged and his pants mended. But as soon as I opened the door he ran past me and curled up in my bed and fell right asleep, the sheets sticking to the bloody spots on his legs.

There were others, too.

I think they're sort of the reason I started throwing things off in the first place. I woke up too early one morning shortly after Neil and I had moved up here. He's a good mechanic and quiet, with a bit of winter in his beard already. He's lived up here since he was eighteen and I know he doesn't have it in him to do what Eddie and Jonah did. He invited me to move in with him after we dated for almost two years. It was a few weeks later that I woke too soon. My eyes opened right away and I realized I hadn't dreamt at all the night before. Nothing I could remember, at least. I slipped out of bed and went outside. We're up so high that sometimes, at the right angles, the sun looks like it recedes forever. That morning I was eye-level with it. I walked toward the cliff about a hundred yards away from the back of the house and when I got near the precipice I looked down and saw a button just at the edge. I worked my big toe under the dirt behind it and lifted up not with speed, but with suddenness, and for that brief moment I felt what little weight there was to the button before it went over. I don't know why I did it. But I felt better. It was as if I was being filled up, to have something so inherently mine.

The next morning, the same thing happened. Only this time I picked up the rock and threw it. It was a loft, just an underhand toss up and over. I grabbed another, bigger this time, and threw that one, too. The thud wasn't inevitable, but by the time the sound reached me it was faint as a light breath. I went back to the house and grabbed some of Neil's change off the dresser, maybe a dollar total. After tossing a few coins individually I walked up and hung my toes over the edge, held out my open hand, and watched the sun hit the money in my palm. As I turned it slowly over, the light hit the divots and crevices of the coins and continued to do so until they fell out of sight.

Now I do it every day, before Neil wakes up. One time I thought he saw me doing it, walking to the edge and throwing some cutlery off, holding my breath as if it helped me hear better, waiting for the tiniest of clangs. It felt as if something had been taken away from me, as if all those old lovers had come back and got what they wanted. I looked over the edge again and wondered what I'd look like on the rocks below, what I'd look like as I went through the air. When I hit, would my eyes be open or closed?

FACTS

The woman in front of me is Czech and timid and naked. She's got flaxen hair down to the arch of her back and a birth certificate that says she's been eighteen for a week. Her name is Zuza. *Graceful lily*. It's what I think of when I photograph her. Bent over a chair: graceful lily. On all fours: graceful lily. Her teeth look to be randomly pasted into her gums, like a sweaty palm with tic-tacs stuck to it, but she's on the less playful side of demure and I don't know how to tell her to smile with her mouth closed and not hurt her feelings. So I tell her to cup her breasts in her hands and grin big: graceful lily.

After she leaves is when I get close. I take the pictures and load them onto the computer, straightening her teeth first and then shading her areolas, making them pinker and puffier. I tone her calves and the shadows they make. I lighten the veins in her ankles. I'm not fixing her, changing the way one bone touches another, but I'm changing the details, changing the facts. I zoom in closer, to the half-moons on her fingernails, and color them a hazy white. It doesn't give the illusion of health any more than oxygen gives the illusion of breathing.

On the picture where she's bent over and looking between her legs, I go to her face and tilt her eyes towards her nose. I own the truth and this is it. I spread her bellybutton, make it look wide and deep. Her shins are tan and I cover them in scars. With a Gaussian blur and the spray-paint tool I can create a skin disease on her elbows, the kind that turns the skin white and flakes outward to the rest of her arm.

The doorbell to my studio rings just as I'm lengthening her earlobes. It's her, Zuza. She forgot her bag. I buzz her up and she's at my door in hardly any time at all.

She comes in and we look for her bag. She walks by my computer while searching and sees the picture of herself, bent over and looking between her legs, covered in defects. "What is this?" she says, the inflection of her English is perfect but hurt, the abnormalities and maladjustments pointed and cutting.

"Look," I start in defense, but nothing more comes out. As if the picture's coming true, Zuza starts rubbing her elbows, her legs, starts following her finger in front of her eyes. "Look," I say again, but still nothing. She's removing her clothes now, not hysterically, but in an even manner, one article at a time that she folds up and sets on a pile on the ground.

She throws her arms up as if defeated. "Take it again."

I've still got nothing to say. I go and grab my camera and hand it to her. "Don't let the truth get the best of you," is all I can think to say. I take off my clothes, too, and stand there across from her. She's confused but she eventually starts shooting me, dozens of the same shot: me in the nude, arms at my side, posture relaxed, eyes focused on the lens.

I walk up to Zuza and replace the camera in her hands with the remote for it. The camera itself I set on the desk chair. I give the chair a spin and run back over to Zuza.

She lets me take her hand and press her thumb with mine, clicking the button on the remote over and over. The chair is still spinning and I give it another twirl. She's clicking on her own now.

I load the pictures onto the computer and we both look at what's been taken, the pictures upon pictures of our bodies, distorted from motion. The dark and light spots of us stretch to lines on the film, the lens trying to capture us as it moves. The time we spend standing here will not be long enough. The computer is buzzing, but still. Zuza is calm. "It feels like waiting," she says, and closes her eyes. I close mine, too, and think: graceful lily.

Sweet Tooth

urt sends mom and dad money each month. They don't need it, but I guess neither does he. That's why I followed him out here to San Diego. I wanted to see how much money he really doesn't need.

I already know how much he has: enough to have the freezer in his basement full of meat from Wisconsin cows, an entire side of beef shipped almost two-thousand miles, four times a year. So right now I'm burning a steak, just getting the grill going as hot as I can on his back porch and then charring a rib-eye. When it's totally black, I'll pitch it into the ocean.

It's Christmas Day and Burt's gone with his family, his wife Nicole and their two daughters, to upstate California. Holidays with the in-laws and I'm watching the house. Fifty bucks a day plus run of the property, a whole acre of beach-front real-estate in San Ysidro. I take his dog, Cale, out for a run in their backyard once or twice a day and then go into town and offer him to strangers, squatters and Mexicans who live twelve, thirteen to an apartment. Nobody ever takes him. If they did, I'd say he ran away on a walk one day, yanked the leash right out of my hand and took off after a truck. Look at the rope burns on my knuckles if you don't believe me, Burt. His daughters would cry until he agreed to buy them a new dog, and then they'd forget about it.

Burt has no problems.

I throw two huge porterhouses on the grill and close the lid.

Back in the house, I mix myself a drink and sit on the sectional in the living room. I sip the drink slow and do an inventory of Burt's possessions. Oil paintings. Lamps made of etched glass and stainless steel. The note he gave me is on the coffee table that matches the lamps. Before he gave it to me, he sent the rest of the family out to the car and waited until the door was closed to say, "If anyone calls, let the machine pick up and erase the messages from these people. I don't give a shit if you call them back, but I wouldn't go blowing all your money on cheap pussy."

Nobody's called yet. Not Gwen or Sheila or Missy or any of them. I've been waiting, though. Waiting and drinking. Vodka and grenadine. A Sweet Tooth is what Burt and I used to call it. It's all we drank when we started out on the booze, Burt thirteen and me fifteen, digging around in the cupboards at home.

The phone rings and I answer it. "Hello?"

"Hey, Burtie baby. What's going on?"

"Who the fuck is this?"

The woman breathes out indignantly and says, "Goddammit, Burt," but I cut her off and start talking into the phone in an even voice, telling her that if I need a warm place to drain my nuts I'll jerk off in a tanning bed, and until I change my mind she can fuck herself.

I set the phone back in the receiver. I want to go to sleep, close my eyes and try to make my head follow them, so I go into Nicole and Burt's room. The bed is king size and has a down comforter covering it, but I go over to the piano against the wall and pull the bench out. It's where Cale likes to sleep, and sure enough he's there, lounging, head on the floor, ears whooshing out from his head. I sit down next to him, right on top of the pedals, and try to go to sleep that way, but I hear something. Carolers. Sleigh bells. They're close and I want to yell at them to shut up. But instead, I reach my hand out in front of me. My fingers curl up over the lip of the piano and the first note I plunk goes perfect with the music. So I plunk it, again and again, until one of us goes away.

What Burns Never Returns

Right now, she's sitting at her kitchen table smelling like the kind of sweat she breaks into after she lights a garbage can on fire, standing too close while empty bags of Cheetos and bottom-tips of waffle cones and beer-bottle caps all melt into one. I'm easily spooked by the unlawful, so I'm never there for it. She shows up later, black hands, the smell of trash soaked into her clothes. But then, a layer deeper, down to the skin over her thighs and ribs, she's pure smoke.

The other things I like about her aren't nearly as plentiful or unclear. Her face is thick and red like a baby's, as if she was grazed on potatoes and lager. I love her like a vacation, like beer hall handouts. Peanuts and pretzels. I tell her this, slowly, like I'm bored or at my wit's end. Really, I'm neither, just looking for clarity but not caring enough to have tact. One strap on her dress is twisted and tight and the other is touching her elbow. She looks like she's waiting to speak and vomit, possibly thinking of a way to combine the two.

I GRAB HER A BEER. I OPEN IT AND SET IT IN FRONT OF HER AND she does nothing. We wait. She leans back and when she stretches her leg out, knocks a matchbook from underneath the table leg. Her full beer wobbles and she stands up. My eyes follow her bust upon movement and we say nothing together for a little bit. When I get to her neck with my eyes, I ask her, "Are you going to hit me?"

She breathes in and out and then says, "Yes."

I take my glasses off and sure enough she lands one right above the left eyebrow. She's a 5'6" southpaw with a wicked haymaker. She walks out the door and I follow her, my eyebrow split to the bone and dripping, though it doesn't hurt much.

SHE'S STANDING ON THE PORCH WITH A LIT CIGARETTE, AND I say to her, "This is your house, you know."

"I know," she says.

I've got one hand over my eyebrow and the other cupped beneath it, already full of blood and dripping over the sides and through the cracks of my fingers, as if I'm a child pausing between scooped drinks from a creek. I'm in the doorway and she's on the steps facing the house, looking like a visitor who doesn't know if she's at the right place. I imagine a few moments from now when this is over and I can't think of her doing anything else than being beneath me, both of us on the disconnected side of content, the cut on my head opening back up and dappling her chest and neck with wispy red droplets of perspiration and blood.

When I step out of the doorway and put both hands on her clavicles, she says, "I've been fucked already. I'm going to bed," and goes back inside. The door doesn't lock, doesn't even close behind her, but I stay where I am, the salt-white of dried sweat plastered on her arms and fading as she moves away from my good eye.

LET'S GO SHOOT HER WHILE SHE'S CRYING

Back when my mother was still alive, I paid some homely intern to write me monthly e-mails detailing new feminist lit releases, which I would then forward to my curious mother under my own name. I saw the girl, Aimee, writing poetry in sea-foam colored ink on her lunch break one day and told her I needed help. Being a woman of youth, she asked why she should help me lie, and being a woman of middle-age, I tried explaining that my mother was a devoted second-waver who raised me to be more like the manager of a women's independent bookstore and less like someone who produces soap operas.

A few minutes into my story, I realized that there's no short way to tell it, that I was just retracing my entire life up to that point—it starts with marches and years later ends with me pleading to a burgeoning poetess near a pile of catered sandwiches. I just told her that there's enough money in the plan for her to afford a new stocking cap or a real haircut, and, to prove I was serious, I opened up her hand and set a fifty-dollar bill in it.

"You think about it. I'll be rearranging the fake plants on the set."

It worked out well for a year or so until my mother had an aneurysm. The neighbors had seen her through the window, motionless on the living room floor, and called an ambulance out of procedural hope. With that, I had lost a mother, but not a friend or confidant, and while my grief certainly existed, it was of the mandatory sort, the self-fulfilling kind I absolutely had to have.

When Aimee sent me the latest reviews a few days later, I told her that her services were no longer needed. She figured it out and sent me an e-mail saying, simply, that she was sorry for my loss. I offered to pay her for the next several months to give her time to adjust to the decrease in income, but she never wrote back, never brought it up again when I saw her. It didn't strike me until later on the set, when Blake smashed a vase of lilies against the ground for the fourth or fifth time, that I had perhaps displayed my personal grieving in the worst possible light.

BOTH ON AND OFF OF THE SET, THE MAIN STARLET IS NAMED Bailey, and both on and off the set she's a sweet girl in her early twenties whose level of self-awareness is inconsistent and confusing. While there are murders and long lost twins to muddle up her life on the show, the biggest tragedy in her real life is that she's pretty enough for daytime television but too plain for movies. She knows this. There's always a new plan to fix her face: change her makeup so her cheekbones pop, add more distance between her eyes, increase the size of her nostrils. She's dating a man who is slightly less glamorous than her, meaning that her list of worries doesn't extend much beyond proper Photo-shopping of her jaw-line-to-eye-socket ratio.

The slightly-less-glamorous boyfriend, Joey, is in a

burgeoning band the crew assumed was just middling enough to be gaining ground commercially, so when a minor part for a coffee house musician came up, Bailey suggested her man and we accepted. Between takes the two of them sat on the floor near catering and he sang her songs. We were waiting for a hair metal ballad, but instead he began playing Beach Boys A-sides and old doo-wop tunes. I was skeptical—"Twenty bucks says 'Living on a Prayer' is next," I told Benny the cameraman—even after everyone had already been convinced.

He comped us a dozen tickets to his band's show that night. The next day, it was all anyone would talk about.

"Where were you?" Bailey asked me during wardrobe.

I kept writing on my clipboard, blocking off scenes, considering the angles. "I was at home. I don't really like live music."

To be kind, I looked up at her as she adjusted herself, fitting her fingers under her bra and giving a slight twist to the left and then right. "I'll bring you one of their albums, then, so you can listen at home."

I never listened to it. I knew it wouldn't be as satisfying as the songs he was playing the day before, a little corny but tender and, at the very least, earnest.

My husband left the week before and I had just started putting bells on the knob of the front door, just started sleeping on the floor in the hallway.

One time, Bailey walked onto the set wearing a dress so black it was almost purple. The lighting team groaned, dropped whispers down upon me.

NOW I SMOKE CIGARETTES, WHICH IS WHAT I WAS DOING when I heard that Bailey was engaged to the musician. I dropped the cigarette on the ground and crushed it with the toe of my flat. "Fantastic. Let's go shoot her while she's crying."

In the show, Bailey's lover had decided to go back with his wife. She was supposed to be a wreck, drinking coffee at 2:00 AM because she can't sleep or leave the house or do anything else. None of the shots looked right. We tried moving her around, changing the lighting, changing her outfit, giving her smelling salts to help her face puff up, but nothing worked. She was glowing, and there wasn't a damn thing we could do about it.

The assistant producer leaned into me and said, "She needs to nail this right fucking now or I'm going to break someone's head against the fake toilet on set nine."

The director cut the scene and I walked over to Bailey, not saying anything, but taking the mug of coffee from her hand and resting it in mine. I hooked my thumb through the handle and set the cup on the tips of my fingers. With my legs crossed, I made sure my posture never faltered, never began to slope as I sat there staring at nothing particular off in the distance, broken and blatant with steam in my face.

I handed the mug back to her. "Like that," I said.

Jests At Scars

ere's how it starts: my son and a girl in his class are rehearsing in my living room as Romeo and Juliet. The balcony scene. The "wherefore art thou Romeo," "a rose by any other name" scene. It's a bit too saccharine and iconic to really mean anything anymore, but the kids don't know that, so their sweetness is genuine, their tension real. She doesn't know what to do with her hands, so she holds onto the script even though she has her lines memorized. My son does the same, curling the script into a tube and then back flat, running the paper ragged with sweat and friction.

I go to my purse to get a stick of gum and when I come back, the traveling musician is playing outside the coffee shop next to my house. Both my house and the shop are of average size and problems, mine mostly structural and the coffee shop's mostly creative writing students loudly emoting. The singer is facing off to the side, leaning slightly in my direction.

He's playing all the sad ones this time. "$1000 Wedding" by Gram Parsons and "Help Me Make It Through the Night" by Kris Kristofferson. He's funny, though, and he does sarcastic versions of "She's No Lady" by Lyle Lovett and "The French Inhaler" by Warren Zevon.

I'm at the window.

I can't tell the story without the metaphor being obvious. It isn't an excuse and it isn't a consolation, because he's gone. There. That's how the story ends.

After he plays for an hour or so, he goes to eat dinner and drink whiskey. When he comes back, I let him spend the night again. The things that I know about him are the things that I don't know about him. He isn't from town, he doesn't play Bob Dylan songs, and there aren't any more people like him left. I don't mean to discredit everyone's individuality, precious a notion as that may be, and there are obviously still people who show up in the street unannounced and begin to play music. Still, to see him do it is to see a sort of archaic approach to feeling that would be better found in the nuances of a caricature of a 1950s alpha male.

The one song he always plays, every time he shows up, is "Changed the Locks" by Lucinda Williams. There's something about it that works against the grain of the constituent parts of my love, and the song has the opposite effect, becomes about the other women who must exist, and I end up leaving the door unlocked that night, any night he shows up. He comes right into my house.

Of course he's not in the bed when I wake up. We all knew better than that. I expected him to leave, but I did not expect to fear the things he left, did not expect to see them everywhere, the bumpy melodies that stretch on and on like the sun on Midwest horizons, breaking through flat and beautiful and then, the climb.

This Illusion

There are exactly four-dozen registered female magicians in the United States and I'm dating one of them. People ask me what it's like to live with her, like she's Bob Dylan and I'm just holding onto her arm on the album cover. In their heads, she regales me with her new tricks when I get home from my job, the unimportant one that doesn't involve real fire or fake telepathy, and when I ask her how it's done she denies me in such a coy way that it only makes me love her more.

The truth is that everything's the same except the laundry, long ropes of scarves mixed in with my t-shirts and a lint trap full of rhinestones.

HER NAME IS RENA. THE NIGHT I MET HER I MISSED HER performance, which was apparently so bad and poorly attended that she walked right off stage and straight to the bar. I thought she was a stripper when I first saw her.

"Really?" she said. "Can you imagine a sexy way to get out of this?" She was wearing something more akin to the outfit of a figure skater, a tight-fitting, low-cut dress made almost entirely of blue and silver sequins and flesh-colored nylon on the chest and arms.

"No, but now I can't unimagine an unsexy way to get

out of it."

Two years go by until a couple at a bowling alley asks us how we met. We tell them the story and the husband says, "Oh boy. And then what happened?"

Rena looks at him. "What do you mean?"

THE PUNS AND JOKES GOT OLD QUICKLY, EVEN WHEN I WAS the one making them. So, outside of using the following words and phrases in their actual context, I've stricken them from my vocabulary: disappearing act, do as I do, you may notice ladies and gentlemen, watch now as.

If I need to say *magic* to Rena about her act, I say *work*. If I need to say *magic* to someone about the way I feel, I don't.

RENA CALLS IT A "FEMALE MAGICIAN CONVENTION" BUT THE reality of it is that it's twenty women hanging out in a hotel suite and showing each other card tricks. I went with her once, not for the cross-country brunch, but for the chance to go somewhere and do something.

We dropped our bags off at our room and then walked up to the suite. All of the other women were already there and they were all beautiful, like models or— and this hit me later—magician's assistants. Rena briefly introduced me to everyone, and as I was leaving I could hear one of them asking her to *tell the story, tell the story*.

"So, what's *the story*?" I asked her that night.

"It's my mentor's story." She didn't sit up, but I leaned onto an elbow and looked at her. "She told me that when she was learning the trade that she kept hearing her mentor say *disillusion* whenever she was actually saying *this illusion*. It made her go on medication for depression."

I go, "Jesus, Rena. Why would they want you to tell that?"

"I tell it to them the funny way. Besides," she finally leaned up on an elbow to face me, "it's not even a true story. I just needed something interesting to tell the girls years ago when we all met, and that came out of my mouth."

She smiled, but it was already in my head: *this illusion meant everything to me, disillusionment: everything to me.*

THE PHONE RINGS AT WORK AND WHEN IT TURNS OUT TO BE for me, nobody is annoyed. I get so few personal calls that I turn into a celebrity of sorts for a few seconds, office carpet as my runway. Cornflower blue is the new black.

It's Rena. Her assistant cancelled for tonight and she wants to know if I can fill in.

"Honey, that's like me asking you to come in here and file the P&L statements because my secretary is sick."

"Do you want me to come file the P&L statements?" She's not a bully, but she has the ears for it, knows from the timbre of a person's voice how much they will or won't do. "Because I will if it means you'll hand me stuff and shuffle a few decks of cards."

When she cuts me in half that night, I swear I can feel it.

WHERE IS YOUR H?

The poetry readings and the town's fascination with the subsequent implosion of the Masterson's marriage would have never happened if I wasn't so bored, so uninterested in the town during the summer. The sexiest baristas had gone home to smaller cities with bigger names—Manitowish, Trempealeau, Oconomawac—and left me with the townies, nice girls who would go on to make thick-legged, weary ex-wives for mechanics and guitarists and dentists. Business dwindled down to a few regulars who wanted distractions more than hot coffee. I'd make fourteen dollars one day, twenty-three the next.

I wasn't trying to facilitate the arts. I just wanted something to do. I expected five or six people to show up, and at first that's what happened. The second week brought a dozen people. The numbers kept doubling. Within six weeks it was standing room only. I served coffee and cappuccino to housewives who read poems about their children and to high schoolers who read poems about how nobody likes the same music as them. It was amusing enough, every bit the small delight I figured it would be. I don't think anyone expected anything of merit or weight, but when we were presented with the public dissolution of love, we turned up in droves, parked our cars miles away if we had to, just for the chance to be able to walk to see it.

Sara Masterson was the one who asked me if she could start up the readings and showed up to the first one with her husband, Billy. They accidentally did it all. He was much older than her and a PhD in something or another, both of which were obvious when they were together: Sara vibrant and high-voiced from speaking to fourth graders all day, Billy sitting down only when necessary and always wearing something made of corduroy. We had no idea how much they despised each other.

At the first reading, Sara read a poem where a woman was a guitar. It was strangled and it screamed and it was allowed none of the credit for the beauty that came from it. Billy read a poem where a man was living under ice, where every time he would speak his words would come out in a thick fog and crash down to the ground in front of him. I wasn't particularly impressed with the work or the sophomoric controlling metaphors, but the Mastersons made it a point to leave early, hand-in-hand, and we all noticed. They returned next week, the crowd almost becoming a crowd. Sara's poem depicted a gravestone that swallowed the intangible pieces of lovers. Billy's poem had two owls, mated for life and miserable because of the tradition. They ran their throats raw and no one was fooled.

The end of summer saw the largest crowd yet. I opened up the area behind the counter to the more trustworthy customers just to make more room. Sara read first, a poem where a snake lived in a tube of wedding rings. We were silent. Billy stood up when she finished, not even bothering to walk up in front of everyone, and began reading a poem we couldn't piece together, one on the history of the letter H. It started as a fence, he said, etched into walls of caves to represent a stop, a partition. He spoke of Sarah, wife of Abraham, mother of Isaac. Woman. Princess. Lady. He moved into his point: though often soundless and voiceless, the H's absence proves an incompleteness. Everyone but Billy looked at Sara as she sat and listened. Billy mused on about the letter, wondering where the letter could be if it was missing. Buried in sand. Drowned in the ocean. Perhaps, he said, perhaps it was never lost. Perhaps it was never there. The grace and stature and the H itself: impossible. He sat and took Sara's hand in his own. Yes, he said. Perhaps. The cappuccino machine made its usual sound, a long sigh, a queue of H's anticipating release.

MYTHOLOGY

Doug has learned to not believe much of what his father-in-law, Frank, says. Lori understands. Her father had certainly been in the Navy, but had never met the Dalai Lama. He had once stopped a man from mugging a woman on the street, but neither, let alone both, had been amputees. He's never seen babies in a harness hanging from a clothesline and he's never seen someone shoot up heroin at a rest stop in Montana.

Doug considered Frank to be semi-dangerous. "Lying is wrong," he said after an instance long ago where Frank tried to convince them that he knows a man who receives a million-dollar check from the government each month. "What if we get married and have kids someday? Do you want them to grow up without a grasp of reality?"

"What's so great about reality?" she said. They were both nineteen and she was two months pregnant. She hadn't told him yet and she was still slender through her stomach, her hips widening only internally.

"What do you mean? It's reality. That's what's so great about it."

She laced her arm through his as they walked to her car. "Is that factual?"

"Yes," Doug said with urgency in his voice. "That's factual."

LORI'S MOTHER HAS DIED IN A NUMBER OF WAYS: KIDNAPPED by Russians, crushed in a bizarre reenactment of the *Challenger* explosion. "Cancer," Lori told Doug when he asked what really happened.

"Oh, that's terrible," he said. "What kind, if you don't mind me asking?"

"Bavarian," she said.

Doug bounced Allie on his knee as she sucked on a popsicle. He shook his head and thought of the injustices of the world, actual abductions and tragedies and cancers. Terror was everywhere all the time. He sighed and his daughter bounded toward Lori.

"One Frank is enough, Lori."

"He likes you. Just let him like you," she said. "Everything's going to be fine." Lori winked at Allie, who started giggling. She handed her mother the popsicle and ran off to play in her room. Lori took a bite and offered the rest to Doug who said no and then, as Lori grinned and kept holding the popsicle in front of him, yes.

ROLLING HER LEGGINGS ON SLOWLY WITH THE FLATS OF HER hands, Lori tries to politely listen to both Doug and her father. Frank is telling a story to the kids and Doug is attempting to speak over him to get the attention of anyone who cares, reciting what time he and Lori will back and detailing each of the emergency phone numbers. The kids are yelling for him to be quiet. Allie's asking Frank what he did after the beautiful woman trained the monkey to steal people's wallets. Her younger brother is repeating the word "wallets" and nodding his head like Allie, and the youngest of all is sitting next to them with a pacifier in his mouth. He looks like Doug when he listens, eyes open and body still.

"Well," Frank starts, leaning back into the couch. He's old, the sort where he could tell someone he's eighty or a hundred or two-hundred years old and they wouldn't doubt it. "I didn't do anything, kiddos. Your dad there did it all. Couldn't believe it myself."

Doug's children turned around to look at him in the doorway. Their mouths were open slightly, even the littlest one, who had taken his binky out of his mouth to gape. "Wow," Allie said. "Then what, dad?" Frank looked at Doug, waiting to hear the rest of the story. Doug saw himself becoming heroic, talking sense into monkeys, throwing himself in front of a firing squad so the beautiful woman can escape her fate and wait for him in America. The guns go off but, somehow, he survives.

B Sharp, C Flat

My son, Jonas, tells me he doesn't want a bike for his tenth birthday. His brother and sister each got one when they turned ten and the surprise is gone, he argues. It's smart and logical, a not-too-deceptive way of telling me that he wants something else, which he soon does, bringing up, of all things, piano lessons.

A trick I learned in the office is to be literally above someone when they're speaking to you, and even though I feel a bit dirty about using it on my nine-year-old son, I wait for him to start talking and then find a reason to get up. I grab a bottle of water out of the fridge and then, not leaning against anything, look down at him looking up at me. He'll look like his mother as he gets older—she has the strong jaw in the family, a charming sort of Gibraltar—but for now he looks like me at that age, thin, almost gaunt around his temples and cheeks, messy brown hair hanging over his ears. The frames of his glasses are sleek and modern but worn down at the temples from constant readjustment. I take the sheet of paper from his hand as he lifts it up to me. Half-hour piano lesson: $15. Hour piano lesson: $25.

I tell him I'll think about it, but as soon as he goes away I think about my first bike instead, bent spokes, no consistent alignment, and broken fenders on both ends rattling against the tires. I press a finger against the backs of my ears and feel a phantom pain from decades ago, my glasses tied to my face with a rubberband so they wouldn't go flying as I dodged branches in the forested hills. I knew I'd miss most of them, but not all of them. It's a numbers game. I get it. Half-hour piano lesson: $15. Hour piano lesson: $25.

MY WIFE, BRENDA DAY, HAS ONE OF THOSE NAMES WHERE everyone, even me, says both parts. When we first met, she couldn't believe how much I used to get in trouble. It was mostly a product of boredom and youthful mischief, mostly minor league versions of big crimes: kidnapping and shaving neighborhood cats, lighting dog houses on fire, breaking into houses and bending all the keys we could find with a pair of pliers. These things still come up every once in awhile, like when I tell her that a bike is better than piano lessons.

She asks me if I think a bike would make it easier for him ride around and spray rose gardens with bleach, which I don't have much of a reply for. She tells me that he doesn't want a bike. Don't get him a bike. He wants piano lessons. "Come on, Brenda Day," I say, but she keeps at it until I lose my train of thought and realize she's standing where I was earlier on in the day and I'm sitting in a chair at the table. Brenda Day's arms are crossed and she's holding a mug of coffee in her left hand. I look down at my feet and then up at her. When I tell her I'll call the music shop tomorrow, she says, "I know," and comes over to kiss me on the top of my head, her hair falling down over my face so all I smell is sweat and lilacs, summer all the time.

JONAS HAS HIS BIRTHDAY AND HIS PIANO LESSONS AND WHEN he goes to bed that night I think I've never seen him more content. The kid doesn't get happy, and I've certainly never seen him overjoyed. He's satisfied with being satisfied. Brenda Day doesn't think it's a problem. "So what?" she says. "We're supposed to be concerned because he can tell the difference between fun and success? Go to sleep."

I go to sleep, and when I wake up a couple hours later, she's still out cold. She turns the air conditioning on extra high so she has a reason to stay close to me, even in the sticky months, and when I wake up, her arms are wrapped loosely around my waist. I wriggle out and when her eyes flutter open, I see the glazed-over whites too tired to be offended. I tuck a firm body pillow in my place and get dressed.

The first thing I do after I grab the neighbor kid's bike is tie a pillowcase onto each handle. Then I ride around collecting all the mirrored gazing balls in the neighborhood. I didn't realize so many people had the stupid things. They don't know that they're only good for that small window when they're shattering against the ground, shards of glass coming up from the concrete like underwater lightning. I climb on top of the school and throw off two and three at a time until I realize I'm running out. When I start to toss them one by one high into the air and watch them fall like a shooting star to the parking lot, I wait for the sound at the bottom, a sound that, by the time it reaches me, is not unlike the most delicate glissando of a piano's highest sharps and flats.

Flood

After three consecutive summers of flooding, the river was finally tame. Those in charge of arranging public events decided in favor of a carnival. Signs were posted around town and advertisements were painted onto the sides of old vans parked in the lots of the pizza place, the gas station. Radio DJs plugged the event between songs. We showed up as a whole and tasted the river in our burgers, smelled it through the smoke.

I spent the day watching Suzie Witthall operate the kissing booth. She worked at the vitamin store and was recently divorced. Though shaped not unlike the other mothers of my youth—hips like parentheses, shoulders stressing into clavicles—she had a sheen of health and a gait that suggested damage. I had turned thirteen a few weeks prior and was uninterested in the girls my age. We were going to be in high school in a matter of months and they too would be reaching toward older loves, seniors and juniors with cars and part-time jobs and problems that seemed more real than those of boys.

Knowing all of this, I was not sorry for staring from a distance, a dollar in my pocket and no nerve to spend it.

THE FOLLOWING YEAR, THE CARNIVAL WAS BACK AGAIN. I

had volunteered to help sell raffle tickets. The men were belligerent by mid-afternoon. Everyone was sweating light beer faster than they could drink it. Anyone with sleeves on their shirt had dark, moist crescents curling up from under their armpits and spidering up their shoulder and chest.

The raffle had ended and many of the prizes remained unclaimed, the winners having either gone home early or shoved their tickets into their pocket and forgotten immediately, not even bothering to check when the numbers were announced. I hadn't thought about Suzie until I was walking the unclaimed prizes to a city van. I saw her leaning over her booth with all her weight on one foot, both elbows on the top of the little plywood surface separating her from the patrons. She looked like a pin-up girl and acted like a stunt double: always ready but bored between the action. A few people had slipped me some tips as a means of showing off, but again I watched Suzie from the sidelines and wondered in units of time, not distance, how much I could get for ten dollars, for a million.

IT FLOODED FOR THE NEXT FIVE YEARS. THE CARNIVAL CAME back and I was living at home after my sophomore year in college. Suzie set the kissing booth back up, and I was old enough to understand what people had thought about her, had always thought about her.

I signed up for nothing and I had no duties or responsibilities of my own. I watched all day as men came up to her and demanded kisses that were slow and hard. They walked away, right past me, bragging to each other about slipping her tongue and pinching her nipple when she leaned over, neither of which were true from my vantage point.

And I had a good vantage point. I saw the reflection off her fingernails as she played solitaire, waiting for men to show up to her booth. She threw the cards she didn't need on the ground and left them there, jacks and aces scattered by her feet. Her clothes were plain but her lipstick glowed like mercury. She reapplied it after every kiss, thick and almost melting, dripping in the heat like a thermometer cracked open and bleeding.

I waited for her to pack up, the grounds crew coming over to disassemble her modest booth, flatten the plywood and cart it off. Everyone left except me was picking up trash. I hopped on my bike and followed Suzie's car from a safe distance, the breeze the night brought with it blowing against my face. I rode slowly down hills, leaning back and lightly holding down the brakes.

It was dark out by the time I got to Suzie's house. There were no lights on anywhere in the neighborhood. My phone began to vibrate and I shut it off. I had married a girl in the fall and ended up divorced by the winter. Everything had moved beyond fast, at a speed that can only be described as sudden. Not just with the girl I had married, but the others, the ones I had wanted to marry and had settled for dating briefly, intensely, for a month, two months. Dozens more didn't even last that long, a weekend at most. I laid my bike and body down at the gate in front of Suzie's house. It was so dark I fell asleep with my eyes open, breathing out in rhythms foreign to my heart.

REFUND

It seems like there's a fucked up kind of Stockholm Syndrome that makes strippers date bouncers. The six or seven times that Rob has seen it happen, the girl traps herself in the job and then, in an odd narcissistic projection, ends up with the person who ensures she maintains the basic right of not having a finger shoved in her ass during a moment of inattentiveness.

Rob's strip club rule #1: Unless she gives the money back, assume she thinks you're a prick.

The bouncers at Razzles are like anyone else in that they have their quirks and charms. Crusher is a germaphobe. Tank spends fifty bucks a week playing pinball. Rob told them he was jealous, that he wanted to date a stripper and have an American Gladiator nickname. He suggested Hammer. They started calling him Ball-peen and, by the time he came back next week, they had convinced the new girl, Minnie, to go ice skating with him at the park. When Rob got there that week and the bouncers introduced them, he shook her hand and wasn't too bad about eye contact. But as she was announced to the main stage, he dumped his beer out under the table and rushed out the front door with dollar bills still balled up in his fist.

RACHEL—MINNIE, AT THE CLUB—IS THE SORT OF BRUNETTE who could turn Hugh Hefner against blondes and Rob's a janitor at Riggston High School a few towns over. They're drunk. It would be one thing if they had too much wine at dinner, but the truth is that they both had the same idea, the same nerves, and showed up already smelling like soda and whiskey, stumbling out of two different cabs at the same time. On the ice they look like two halves of the same bird, Rachel the graceful wings and Rob the awkward, dangling feet. It doesn't take long for them to wear out, and they end up sitting on a bench after about five minutes. A group of men in dark Carhartt jackets are standing nearby looking at blueprints some of the time and Rachel most of the time. At one point, they begin laughing like dads on a sitcom, a slight leaning back of the head and a bouncing chuckle. Every time Rob tells a joke, he looks to Rachel's mouth, hoping to see the giant ball of steam that covers her entire face when she laughs for real.

THEY'RE IN THE BAR OF A MARRIOTT NEAR THE ICE RINK, making sure they don't end up sober. She orders shots of tequila. "I haven't had shots since I was nineteen," Rob tells her.

"How old are you?" She leans forward as if watching a scary movie, anticipating the worst: *I'm thirty-six or forty-five or fifty-two. I collect social security and am in immeasurable pain right now because I'm not sitting on my hemorrhoid donut.*

He tells her that he's twenty-eight and she considers it while trying to look like she's not considering it. It means she's not as drunk as she'd like to be, and when she finally says, "Really?" it means that neither is Rob. They do the shots and then she goes, "I'm nineteen. But I'm old enough to know what you're trying to do."

Other than her looks, that statement is the only thing about her so far that's interested him. Now he's the one leaning forward waiting for the punchline, the gunshot and camera zoom.

"You've been trying really hard all night not to ask me about stripping so that when I bring it up we can talk about it all you want. And then!" She raises her finger in the air like an infomercial. "You can tell me you don't care that I'm a stripper and I'll feel great and you'll be different than everyone else I've ever met and we'll be happy. Right?"

She's trying to catch him in a lie he never told, which leaves the same kind of smirk on her face, and, thus, reminds Rob of lies he actually has told. "Look," he tells her. "After awhile, life becomes technical college. You can't be anything you want to be. You can be, like, twenty things. That's it."

And with that she grew quiet, possibly considering what he had said, but more likely inherently understanding it and instead considering the loudest boys in the loudest clubs yelling up at her, her skin like diamonds under wet glass.

At the point between the end of the night and the start of the morning, they find themselves in a churchyard. The sun is coming up slowly behind one of them and then the other as they make opposing laps around the courtyard, their balance only slightly better than a half dozen odd hours ago on the ice. They pass each other at two opposing points in the circle, and when they do she talks about how it's too much like a movie, too much like perfection. Rob has his own reasons to run, but when she stops him and puts her hands on the lapels of his jacket, he sees no difference between right and right now.

Things That Are Glacial,
Things That Are Gone

Someone mentions the end of the world, casually, as if it's a television show or a sandwich. You think about buying a life insurance policy even though the only thing you can afford to do is die.

Everyone has said something about the end of the world, the unfortunate eventuality of it, except you. This is what camping is: drink near something that's green and something that's on fire and say absurdly plain things about nature and love and death. The only thing you can think to do is list contextually-accurate irrational fears you are currently harboring, mainly the one about how every living thing is in a constant state of expansion pulling so slowly and smoothly away from itself that we will become transparent and malleable to a point where identity is negligible, a matter of whose cells are tangled up in whoever else's cells.

Instead of saying that, you take a breath and hold it. It knocks against your teeth before settling into your soft palate, next to the names of those you've licked tenderly on the stomach and thighs, the ones who had considered friction a good idea and threw box fans and box cutters, one and then the other, until problems were solved or replaced with bigger problems. Your tongue becomes restless and you think of mothers everywhere either naming sons or being buried by them. All three—the mothers and sons and dogs—end up in the earth beneath your feet. You decide: before the world ends, you will date an academic, a geologist with attractive ex-spouses and several pairs of eyeglasses. One night after a failed dinner party, you will ask if certain areas of the earth are called driftless because of something that has left or because of something that was never there. *Wait,* you'll say, *don't tell me.* You'll pretend to think hard and then you'll change the subject.

People aren't talking about the end of the world anymore. Now people are talking about the beginning of the world. You're still holding your breath. The buzzwords are the same as always—God, higher power, Darwin, creationism, monkeys—and boiled down to those essentials you realize that you are in the woods with people you don't even like, the sort of people who give birth to twins and name one of them Denim and one of them Lace, the sort of people who squeeze toothpaste from the middle and consult *Consumer Reports* without feeling silly.

If you weren't still holding your breath, you would look at the person directly across from you and tell her that you don't even like her. Instead, you just look at the person directly across from you. You think of breathing out, that momentary light-headed feeling that happens before your blood falls back into place, moving down through your feet and toes, unaware of how hard and in what direction it pounds.

Now no one is saying anything.

Acknowledgments

THANKS TO MY MOTHER, WHO STILL DOES MY LAUNDRY. Also, my father, who is very reasonable when complaining about my mother still doing my laundry.

THIS BOOK WOULD HAVE BEEN MADE POSSIBLE WITHOUT SAM Snoek-Brown, but it would have been a pretty shitty book. Excluding his fashion sense, we'd all be better people if we were a bit more like Sam.

IN ADDITION TO FINDING REALLY NICE WAYS TO TELL ME TO shut the fuck up and chill out, Mike Sweeney did a lot of work in editing this thing together into a state of coherency.

EIRIK GUMENY PRETTY MUCH LET ME DO WHATEVER I wanted. Dudes in charge don't get much cooler.

TO THOSE WHO DONATED TO THE KICKSTARTER FUND FOR THIS book: THANK YOU.

KATIE DUFFY DESIGNED THE BOOK AND SAID MEAN THINGS TO me, two things she did a very good job with.

EARLY INSPIRATION AND GUIDANCE IS CREDITED TO DEB Lewis, Stormy Stipe, Paula Neuhaus, and their respective writing workshops.

THANKS TO NJE FOR "MONSTERS."

THANKS TO REDHEADS—JUST BECAUSE.

All of these stories are based on songs, most of them suggested by writers and musicians from around the world. Without them, there is no book.

"Back and to the Left" is based on "Brain of J" by Pearl Jam , as suggested by writer Stephen Schwegler; "Sergei Avdeyev" is based on "Traveller In Time" by Uriah Heep, as suggested by musician Mike Conte of the band Early Man; "Look At How Fast I Can Go Nowhere At All" is based on "Life Passed Me By" by Super Stereo, as suggested by writer Monica Rodriguez; "The King" is based on "Do Anything You Wanna Do" by Thin Lizzy; "Plots" is based on "Transatlantic Foe" by At the Drive-In, as suggested by musician Philip Chavez; "Wide Right Game" is based on "Helps Both Ways" by Mogwai; "When There Is No Road" is based on "Rock N Roll" by Paleface, as suggested by musician Monica "Mo" Samalot of Paleface; "It's Been Far Too Long Since You Woke Up In Someone Else's Shoes" is based on "Misunderstood" by Wilco; "Monsters: A Series of Non-Linear Vignettes" is based on "Snow & Lights" by Explosions In the Sky; "Rust" is based on "Your Friend and Mine—Neil's Song" by Love, as suggested by musician Bob Bucko Jr.; "The Vikings" is based on "Smoke on the Water" by Deep Purple, as suggested by musician Kristian Dunn of El Ten Eleven; "Signal" is based on "Have a Cigar" by Pink Floyd, as suggested by writer Don Balch; "--:--" is based on "The Beginning and the End" by ISIS; "Haunt" is based on "Ghosts of the Garden City" by Caspian, as suggested by musician Philip Jamieson of Caspian; "After I Threw the Ball At Thomas Hernandez and Before It Killed Him" is based on "Jesus Christ" by Brand New, as suggested by writer Adam Gallari. (Mojo lovingly borrowed from Dave Eggers); "Follow the Water" is based on "New Kind of Kick" by The Cramps, as suggested by writer yt sumner; "A Few Thoughts On Bloodlines" is based on "Cure For Pain" by Morphine; "Focus" is based on "Hyperballad" by Björk, as suggested by writer Benjamin Rosenbaum; "Facts" is based on "Crosseyed and Painless" by Talking Heads, as suggested by writer Kirk Nesset; "Sweet Tooth" is based on "I Wanna Be Your Dog" by The

Stooges, as suggested by musician Ted Nesseth of The Heavenly States; "What Burns Never Returns" is based on "Alcoholiday" by Teenage Fanclub. (Title stolen from Don Caballero); "Let's Go Shoot Her While She's Crying" is based on "Black Coffee" by Sarah Vaughan, as suggested by writer Dena Rash Guzman; "Jests At Scars" is based on "Hard-core Troubadour" by Steve Earle; "This Illusion" is based on "Feel" by Big Star; "Where Is Your H?" is based on "Smile & Wave" by Headstones, as suggested by writer Tim Trenkle; "Mythology" is based on "Bullet and a Target" by Citizen Cope, as suggested by writer Keith Scribner; "B Sharp, C Flat" is based on "Bicycle Bicycle, You Are My Bicycle" by Be Your Own Pet, as suggested by writer Kevin Wilson; "Flood" is based on "Sad Eyed Lady of the Lowlands" by Bob Dylan, as suggested by musician Patrick Fleming of The Poison Control Center; "Refund" is based on "On To You" by The Constantines, as suggested by musician Kevin J. Frank of Haymarket Riot; "Things That Are Glacial, Things That Are Gone" is based on *Adagio For Strings* by Samuel Barber, as suggested by writer/nuisance Stephanie Momot

About the Author

Depending on when you are reading this, Ryan Werner is either working a shitty job in the Midwest or is dead.

Ryan Werner (Writes Stuff)
www.ryanwernerwritesstuff.com